THE GREAT HUNTER

by Lyn Gray

Published by NyreePress Publishing

a division of NyreePress Literary Group

NyreePress books may be ordered through booksellers or by contacting:

Bug Love Books
an imprint of NyreePress Publishing
a division of "NyreePress Literary Group" (972) 793-3736
www.nyreepress.com

Illustrated by Jamie Cosley
www.jamiecosley.com

ISBN: 978-0-615-76536-5
Children's Fiction/Fiction

NyreePress

printed in the United States of America

I am Annie, The Great Hunter, and I am stalking my prey. I should be able to find at least a tiger or an elephant in this jungle.

Hmmm. What do I see? Footprints?
Wow, they're huge! Must be an elephant.

I think I will
crouch down
and creep up
behind it.

SNIFF
SNIFF

Augh! The footprints suddenly faded away.

Now, I don't see an elephant anywhere.

Let's see. If I continue trudging through the forest in this direction, I just might find something.....

...anything.

The Great
Hunter
can NOT
go back
empty
handed.

Hmmm. What's behind those bushes?

The tiger beats
a hasty retreat.

Wait a minute! Why did I do that?
I wanted to take my prize home.
I got so excited, I forgot.
Oh well......

Oh, now Great Hunter, you'd better pay attention.
You need to find a foe and take it down.

Remember, you want to drag it back to the village to show the people what a great hunter you are. You can't do that if you scare it away.

Continue to stalk, tromp, tromp, up and down, down and up.

back and forth,

forth and back.

As I lay my head down on my paws, I suddenly hear something.

Hmm. What is it? It's coming this way!

Steady, steady. Don't move yet.
Keep your eyes on it. But don't move yet.
Wait for it!

Wait for it! It's soooooooooo hard for me to wait!

NOW!!!! You can get it!!
Leap with your jaws open!!

Hey, where'd the ground go?

Gosh....I jumped....and fell right off.....

...the bed!

What was I going after?
Oh, it was just a fly.

The Great Hunter was chasing a fly?!

And didn't get it because
she fell off the bed?

How embarassing!

Don't tell anybody, ok?

It will just be our little secret, ok?

Thanks!

CPSIA information can be obtained at www.ICGtesting.com
Printed in the USA
LVOW02s1652220813

349042LV00004B/5/P

9 780615 765365